bunny

CRACKERS

For my brother, Alan, who also ran away —K.M.C.
For Johny —L.C.

Text copyright © 2010 by Kenneth M. Cadow
Pictures copyright © 2010 by Lauren Castillo
Distributed in Canada by D&M Publishers, Inc.
Color separations by Chroma Graphics PTE Ltd.
Printed in October 2009 in China by SNP Leefung Printers Ltd.,
Dongguan City, Guangdong Province
Designed by Irene Metaxatos
First edition, 2010
1 3 5 7 9 10 8 6 4 2

www.fsgkidsbooks.com

Library of Congress Cataloging-in-Publication Data
Cadow, Kenneth M.
    Alfie runs away / Kenneth M. Cadow ; pictures by Lauren Castillo.— 1st ed.
        p.   cm.
    Summary: Told he must give up his favorite, now too-small, shoes, Alfie leaves
home, but not before his mother persuades him to take all of the things he might
need while he is gone.
    ISBN: 978-0-374-30202-3
    [1. Runaways—Fiction.   2. Mothers and sons—Fiction.]   I. Castillo, Lauren, ill.
II. Title.

PZ7.C117245 Alf 2010
[E]—dc22

                                                                      2008024146

ALFIE
RUNS AWAY

Kenneth M. Cadow
Pictures by Lauren Castillo

Frances Foster Books • Farrar Straus Giroux • New York

Alfie did not like to take baths.
He did not like to make his bed.
He did not like to set the table.
And he did not like to eat potatoes.
But now things had gone too far.
His mother wanted to give away his favorite shoes.

Alfie took his blanket and his little pillow.
He put his favorite shoes on his feet.
"I am going to run away," he told his mother.

"Oh, Alfie," said his mother.
"Don't run away in those shoes.
They are too small for you."

"They are not too small for me,"
said Alfie. "I am running away."

"If you run, you might be thirsty," said his mother.
"Would you take a water bottle with nice cold water?"
She filled a big water bottle at the sink.
Alfie took a sip from the water bottle.
"Goodbye," he said.

"Do you think you will need a flashlight?" asked his mother.
"The nights are very dark."
Alfie took a flashlight.

"Do you think you will need extra
batteries?" asked his mother.
"The nights are very long."
So Alfie took two extra batteries.

Alfie dropped the flashlight.
"Whoops," he said.
When he picked it up, he dropped the batteries.
"Whoops," he said.
But when he picked up the batteries,
he dropped the water bottle.

"I think you will need a bag," said his mother.
She brought Alfie a very big bag.
"You can put your blanket and your little pillow
in there, too," said his mother.

Alfie put the flashlight and the batteries in the bag.
He put his little pillow and his blanket in the bag.
He put his water bottle in the bag.

"Do you think you will want to eat?" asked his mother.

"I will *have* to eat," said Alfie.

Alfie's mother opened the pantry.

She gave him a jar of peanut butter and some crackers.

He put them in his bag.

She gave him a big box of raisins.
"I don't like raisins," said Alfie.
She put the raisins back in the pantry.

"Goodbye," said Alfie.
"I will miss you," said his mother.
"I want to keep my shoes," said Alfie.

"Do you think your Buddy Bear
will miss you, too?" asked his mother.
Alfie went to his room.
Buddy Bear was nestled on his bed.
He took the bear and put it in the bag.

"Do you think you will want some books to read?" asked his mother.
"You can read to Buddy Bear the same way I read to you."

Alfie liked that idea.
He picked three books.
He picked a book about a bunny.
He picked a book about a bear.
And he picked a book about a toad and a frog.
He put the books in his bag.

"May I give you a hug?" asked his mother.

"You may let me keep my shoes," said Alfie.

"I will put a hug in your bag," said his mother,
and she put her arms in the bag.

"You are being silly," Alfie said.

He put the bag on his back.

His mother opened the door.

"Be careful out there, Alfie," she said.

"Goodbye," said Alfie.

Alfie stepped onto the back porch
and he went down the stairs.
His mother shut the door behind him.

He walked away from the house
and far into the backyard.
The bag was very, very heavy.
Alfie's back hurt.

He took a deep breath.
He slipped the bag off his back and opened it up.
He pulled out his blanket and spread it on the grass.

Alfie set his pillow on the ground
and leaned Buddy Bear against it.
He made some peanut butter crackers
and took a drink of water.

Alfie did not need his flashlight yet.
He set it with the extra batteries
on one corner of the blanket.

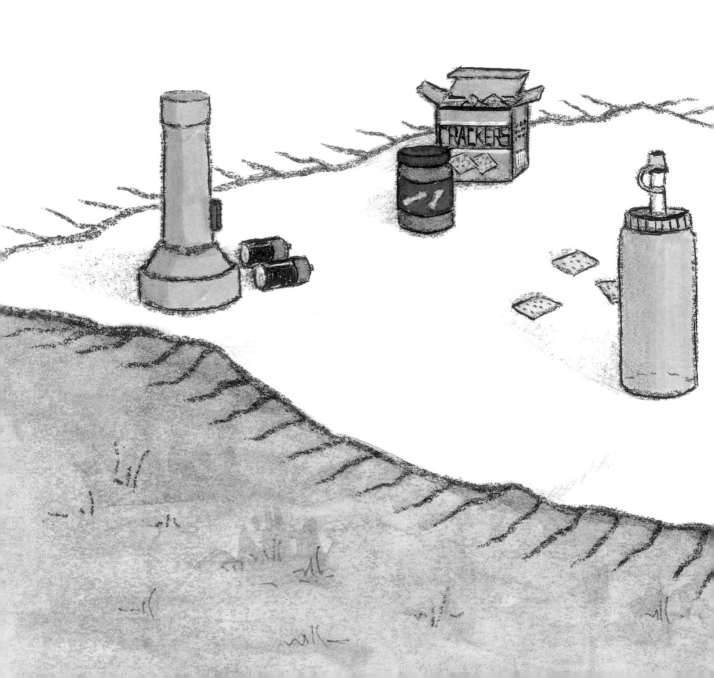

The sun was strong.
Alfie's feet were hot and sore.
He took off his shoes
and put them on Buddy Bear.

Alfie stuck his toes into the cool grass.
He put his head in his bear's lap
and looked up at the blue sky.

Alfie yawned.
"Would you like me to read to you?"
he asked Buddy Bear.
Alfie opened a book and looked at the pictures.

Alfie yawned again.
He looked at his bear.
"You're very sleepy too, aren't you?" he asked.
"Do you miss snuggling in our bed?"
The bear waited.

The sun passed behind the trees.
Alfie felt chilly.
He looked in the bag to see
if a hug was really there.
There was no hug.
He looked back at the house.

His mother was crossing the lawn.
Her arms were spread open wide.

"She's coming with the hug," Alfie said.
He looked at Buddy Bear.
"Don't worry," he said.
"We don't have to run away forever.
Those shoes will never get too small for you."